D0319844

Disney
PRINCESS

This edition published by Parragon Books Ltd in 2017

Parragon Books Ltd
Chartist House
15–17 Trim Street
Bath BA1 1HA, UK
www.parragon.com

ISBN 978-1-5270-0739-0

Printed in China

Enchanting Storybook Collection

Parragon

Bath • New York • Cologne • Melbourne • Delhi
Hong Kong • Shenzhen • Singapore

Contents

7 Cinderella

77 The Little Mermaid

147 Beauty and the Beast

Disney
PRINCESS
Cinderella

Once upon a time, there lived a beautiful girl called Cinderella. Her mother had died when she was very young so Cinderella lived alone with her father. She loved her father dearly but he knew that his daughter needed a mother, so he married again. Cinderella's stepmother had two daughters of her own, Drizella and Anastasia.

But when her father died suddenly, a broken-hearted Cinderella quickly discovered that her stepmother, Lady Tremaine, was cold, cruel and bitterly jealous of Cinderella's charm and beauty.

As time went by, Cinderella became a servant in her own home. Yet, every morning she found new hope that someday her dreams of happiness would come true. Despite how her stepfamily treated her, Cinderella always remained gentle and kind. Her many devoted animal friends helped her to get dressed each day.

One morning, Jaq the mouse rushed in to tell Cinderella that a new mouse was caught in a trap! Cinderella hurried down to the cellar to rescue him.

"The poor little thing is scared to death!" Cinderella said. "Jaq, maybe you'd better explain things to him."

Jaq befriended the new mouse and Cinderella gave him a shirt, shoes, cap – and a name. "We'll call you Gus," she said.

Gus giggled his approval.

Among her many chores, Cinderella had to go to the farmyard to feed the chickens. The mice always followed her because Cinderella saved some corn for them every day.

But today, Lady Tremaine's mean old cat, Lucifer, was blocking their way! The mice drew tails to see who would distract Lucifer so the others could run outside.

It was up to Jaq! He quietly crept up to Lucifer and kicked the cat's leg out from under him. **Splash!** Lucifer slipped face down into his milk bowl and the mice scurried past and out into the farmyard.

Cinderella had been wondering where the mice were. "Breakfast is served," she said when they appeared, and she scattered plump kernels of corn on the ground for them.

Cinderella spent the rest of her day attending to chores.

"Take that ironing," Drizella demanded.

"Don't forget to make our tea," Anastasia added.

"Pick up the laundry and get on with your duties," her stepmother ordered.

Meanwhile, at the royal palace, the King complained to the Grand Duke. "It's high time my son got married," he sobbed. "I want grandchildren!"

The King decided to hold a ball. "If all the eligible maidens come," said the King, "the Prince is bound to find his bride among them."

Later that morning, Cinderella paused from her chores to answer a knock at the door. A palace messenger handed her an invitation to the ball for that very evening.

Her stepmother grabbed the invitation and read it aloud. "By royal command, every eligible maiden is to attend," she said.

Her daughters squealed with excitement.

"I'm so eligible!" said Anastasia.

They both imagined the Prince would fall in love with them.

Cinderella was also excited. "Why, that means I can go, too!" she said.

The stepsisters laughed. "Every eligible maiden is supposed to attend," said Cinderella.

Surprisingly, her stepmother agreed. "I don't see why you can't go ... *if* you get all your work done, and *if* you can find something suitable to wear."

Cinderella raced to her room and found a dress that had belonged to her mother. With a little stitching, she knew she could make it pretty.

As Cinderella worked on the dress, her stepmother and stepsisters called for her and gave her a long list of chores to do.

Meanwhile, the mice and the birds retrieved some sashes and beads that the stepsisters had thrown away. With some clever stitching and folding, they turned Cinderella's simple dress into a fabulous ballgown!

Cinderella finally finished her chores and went up to her room. She was so sad when she saw how late it was and realized she had no time to mend her dress before the ball. She gazed out of the window. In the distance, she could just make out the long line of carriages arriving at the palace for the ball.

Then, out of the corner of her eye, Cinderella saw her new dress.

"Surprise!" yelled the mice and birds.

"Oh, thank you so much!" Cinderella cried with delight.

When Anastasia and Drizella saw Cinderella looking so beautiful in their old sashes and beads, they flew into a jealous rage.

They ripped Cinderella's dress, pulling off the sashes and yanking the beads, while Lady Tremaine just stood and watched.

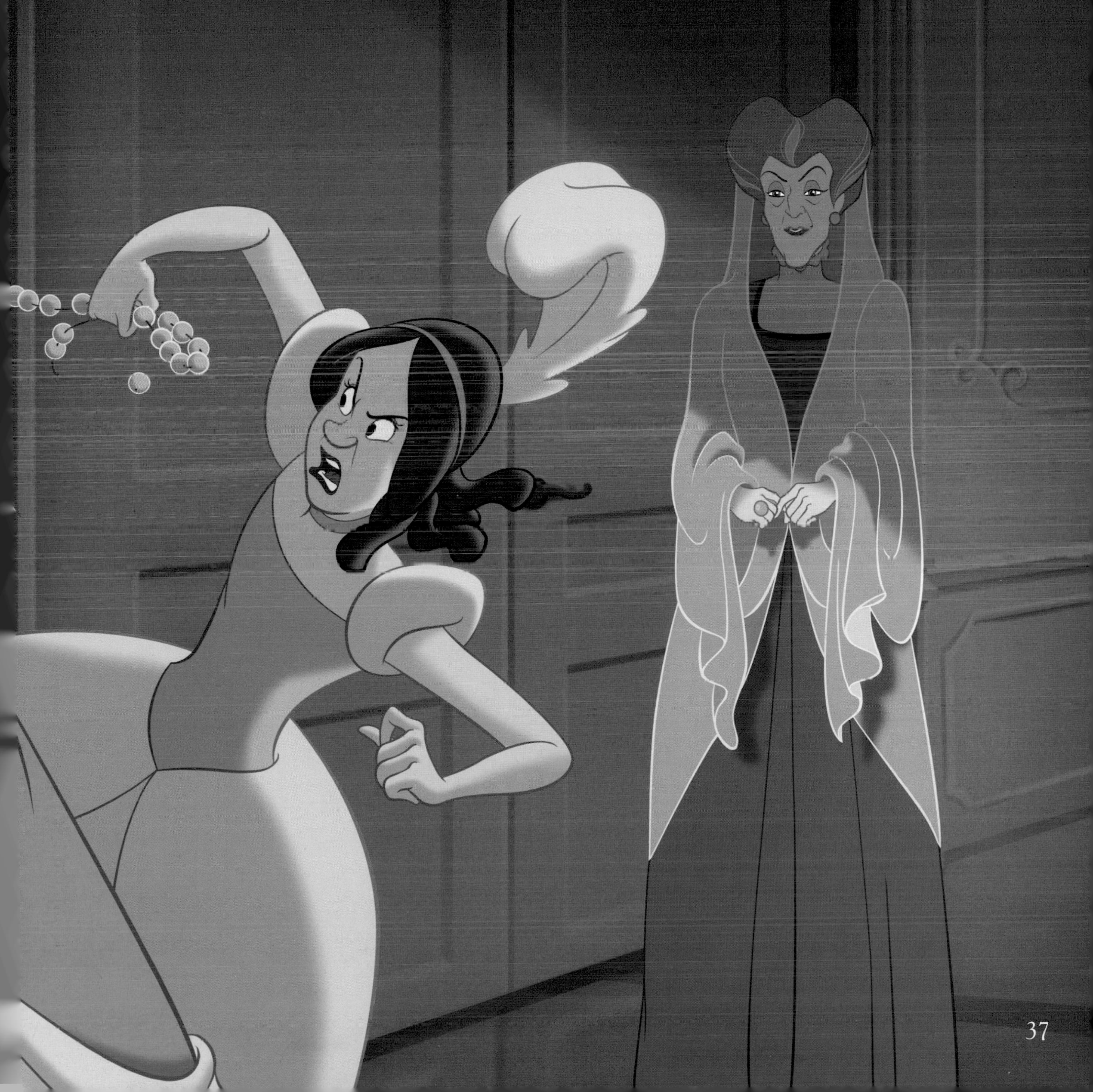

Now Cinderella had no hope at all of making it to the ball. She ran to the garden and sobbed. "There's nothing left to believe in," she said, "nothing."

But just then, a comforting presence appeared beside her – it was Cinderella's Fairy Godmother. "Dry those tears," she told Cinderella. "You can't go to the ball looking like that."

"But I'm not going," said Cinderella.

"Of course you are," replied the Fairy Godmother.

The Fairy Godmother waved her magic wand over a pumpkin and a regal coach appeared!

"Oh, it's beautiful," said Cinderella.

Then the Fairy Godmother turned Jaq and Gus and two other mice into four beautiful white horses. She changed Major the horse into the coach driver and Bruno the dog into the footman.

The Fairy Godmother waved her wand again and said "Bibbidi-bobbidi-boo!" With that, she turned Cinderella's torn dress into a beautiful gown. Then a pair of dainty glass slippers appeared on Cinderella's feet.

"On the stroke of midnight, the spell will be broken," the Fairy Godmother warned, "and everything will be as before."

Cinderella raced to the palace in her magical carriage, her friends carrying her as fast as they possibly could.

Every maiden at the ball came forward in turn to meet the Prince, including Anastasia and Drizella.

The sisters curtsied before the Prince but he was not looking at them – he had noticed Cinderella standing behind them.

The Prince hurried over to Cinderella, eager to meet the most beautiful girl he had ever seen.

They talked for a while and then the Prince led Cinderella into the ballroom.

They danced and danced, gazing deeply into each other's eyes ... the two were falling in love.

But suddenly the clock began to strike midnight. **Bong! Bong!**

"I must go!" Cinderella cried in panic, freeing her hand from the Prince's.

As she fled, she lost one of her glass slippers on the staircase.

Cinderella jumped into her waiting carriage. They were a short distance from the palace when the clock finished striking. Everyone and everything turned back to normal! But Cinderella still had one glass slipper. She looked up and thanked her Fairy Godmother for a magical evening.

Back at the Palace, the Prince vowed that he would marry the girl who had lost her glass slipper at the ball.

The King was furious that the girl his son now loved had vanished and nobody seemed to know who she was. He demanded that the Grand Duke go and find her.

A royal messenger brought news of the search to Lady Tremaine. She read the notice aloud – the Prince would marry whoever fitted the glass slipper. Anastasia and Drizella were excited to have another chance to marry the Prince.

Cinderella overheard her stepmother reading the royal message and ran to her room, not quite believing what she had heard. The Prince had fallen in love with her, just as she had fallen in love with him! But Lady Tremaine realized that it must have been Cinderella who had lost the slipper. She went up to Cinderella's room ...

… and locked the door!

“Let me out!” Cinderella cried.

But her stepmother put the key in her pocket and left.

The Grand Duke travelled the kingdom on behalf of the King, searching for the owner of the glass slipper. When he arrived at Lady Tremaine's house, she and her daughters hurried to greet him.

Meanwhile, Jaq and Gus had seen what the stepmother had done to Cinderella. So, while she was talking to the Grand Duke, they sneaked up and stole the key from her pocket!

They took it back to Cinderella and slid it under her door.

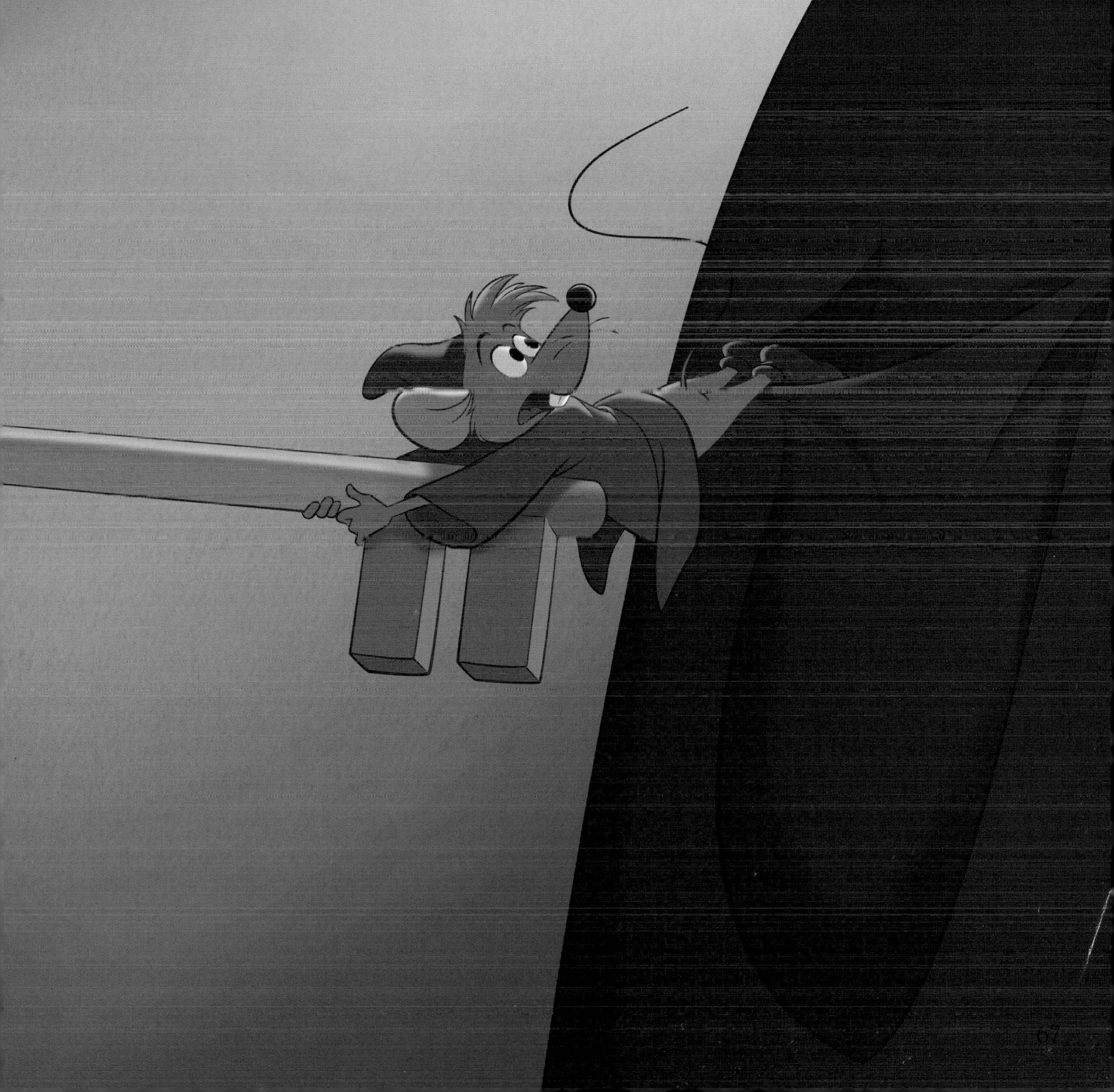

The Grand Duke looked on as his footman tried to squeeze Anastasia's and Drizella's huge feet into the delicate little slipper.

Of course, it did not fit either of them.

Just as the Grand Duke was about to leave, Cinderella appeared at the top of the stairs. Her animal friends had freed her just in time!

"May I try on the slipper?" she asked.

The angry stepmother tripped the footman as he approached Cinderella. The glass slipper shattered on the floor.

"Oh, no!" moaned the Grand Duke.

"But you see," said Cinderella, reaching into her pocket, "I have the other slipper." Quickly, the Grand Duke put the slipper on Cinderella's foot.

It fitted perfectly! Cinderella was the Prince's love!

A royal wedding was quickly arranged and Cinderella and the Prince were married, to the delight of the King and all of Cinderella's animal friends.

Disney
PRINCESS
THE LITTLE
MERMAID

Deep under the sea, merfolk and sea creatures hurried to King Triton's glittering palace. Ariel, his youngest daughter, was making her musical debut in a special concert and no one wanted to miss it!

King Triton arrived as everyone gathered in the great hall. With a tap of his baton, Sebastian, the court composer, instructed the orchestra to begin. But when the time came to introduce Ariel ... she wasn't there!

Ariel had forgotten about the concert. She was miles away, searching for human treasures in a sunken ship.

Her friend Flounder followed her nervously around the ship.

"Have you ever seen anything so wonderful in your entire life?" Ariel asked her friend, picking up a silver fork.

"Yeah, it's great," Flounder muttered. "Now let's get out of here!"

Suddenly, a huge mouth of teeth appeared behind them.

"A shark! Swim!" Flounder shouted.

The two friends swam for their lives as the shark charged after them. As the shark leaped forward to take a big bite it got stuck tight in an old anchor.

"Take that, you big bully!" Flounder taunted.

Ariel and Flounder swam to the surface to find Scuttle, a seagull who claimed to know all about the human world.

Scuttle examined the fork. “This is a dinglehopper,” he said. “Humans use these to comb their hair.”

Just then, Ariel remembered the concert.

“My father’s going to kill me!” she gasped.

In a cave, a sea witch called Ursula used her magic to watch Ariel hurry home.

She laughed to herself as she thought of her plan to use Ariel to get back at King Triton.

When King Triton learned that Ariel had missed the concert because she had been to the surface, he was furious. He believed humans were dangerous and he wanted to protect her.

"You are never to go to the surface again!" he commanded.

After Ariel left, King Triton asked Sebastian to keep an eye on her.

Sebastian followed Ariel to a secret grotto. When he peeked inside, he was stunned to see that it was filled with human treasures.

The little crab was shocked to overhear Ariel tell Flounder how much she wanted to be part of the human world.

Sebastian tried to talk some sense into Ariel, but she didn't want to listen. Before he could stop her, Ariel swam to the surface again – to watch a large ship sail past.

Peeking through a hole in the side of the ship, Ariel saw Prince Eric. He was smiling as his guardian, Sir Grimsby, unveiled a statue of him. Ariel couldn't stop gazing at Eric.

Scuttle saw Ariel as he flew past and joined her as she spied on Eric.

"He's very handsome, isn't he?" she asked Scuttle.

Suddenly, thunder roared and lightning cracked as a storm hit. A lightning bolt struck the ship and set it on fire.

As the fire burned, the ship was rocked by huge waves. Ariel watched in horror as Eric was thrown overboard and swept into the sea.

Beneath the waves, Ariel grabbed the unconscious prince. Struggling to keep hold of him, she pulled him to safety on the shore.

While Scuttle listened for a heartbeat, Ariel sang to him in a clear, beautiful voice. But when she heard people approaching she dived quickly back into the sea.

As Eric woke up he only caught a glimpse of her face, but he knew he would never be able to forget her voice.

Ariel was in love and all she could do was think about Eric. Her father noticed her strange behaviour and asked Sebastian to take him to Ariel.

At the entrance of her grotto, King Triton watched as his love-struck daughter sang about a human!

Furious, Triton burst in. "Contact between the human world and merworld is forbidden!"

"But, Daddy, I love him!" announced Ariel.

"If this is the only way to get through to you, then so be it!" Triton shouted as he raised his trident.

Flashes of light filled the room and the statue of Eric and the rest of Ariel's treasures were destroyed.

Upset with her father, Ariel went to Ursula's cave. The sea witch offered to turn Ariel into a human – if she could keep Ariel's voice.

The deal also meant that Eric had to kiss her before sunset on the third day.

"If not, you'll turn back into a mermaid and belong to me!" Ursula cackled.

Frightened but determined, Ariel signed the contract.

"Now, sing!" Ursula commanded.

Ariel's voice flowed from her and Ursula captured it in a seashell.

Suddenly, Ariel began to transform and her tail disappeared. In its place, she had legs.

Flounder and Sebastian helped Ariel to the surface, where she looked at her new legs, delighted.

Sebastian was worried about Ariel and agreed to help her, along with her friends, in the human world.

Just as Ariel's friends helped her to the shore and dressed her in an old ragged sail, the prince and his dog appeared and spotted her.

"You look familiar," Eric told Ariel. Was she the girl who sang to him? But when Eric realized that Ariel couldn't talk, he decided she couldn't be the girl he was looking for.

Eric took Ariel back to his palace where she was dressed in a beautiful ball gown and invited to dinner.

To the prince's surprise Ariel combed her hair with a fork, just as Scuttle had taught her. Sebastian hid himself at the dinner table so that he could keep an eye on Ariel.

The next day, Eric took Ariel on a tour of his kingdom. Despite the fun they had, Eric still had not kissed her and there was only one day left!

At sunset, the prince took Ariel rowing on a lagoon. Sebastian – with the help of the others – sang a song about love. Eric gazed at Ariel, but just as they were about to kiss the boat was tipped over by eels that had been sent by Ursula.

Ursula used her magic to watch from her cave.

"That was too close," she said to herself. "It's time I took matters into my own hands."

Ursula then transformed herself into a beautiful young woman named Vanessa. She wore a necklace with the shell that contained Ariel's voice.

When Ariel woke up the next day, she rushed downstairs to see Eric announce his marriage to Vanessa.

Ariel was heartbroken. She had lost her true love and now she would never escape Ursula's clutches.

"The wedding ship departs at sunset," Eric told Grimsby.

Once aboard the ship Ursula gloated. She had managed to trick the prince using Ariel's beautiful singing voice and had put him under a spell. Soon, Ursula would rule the sea!

Ursula didn't notice that Scuttle had seen her talk about her plan through a porthole. He saw her true reflection in the mirror.

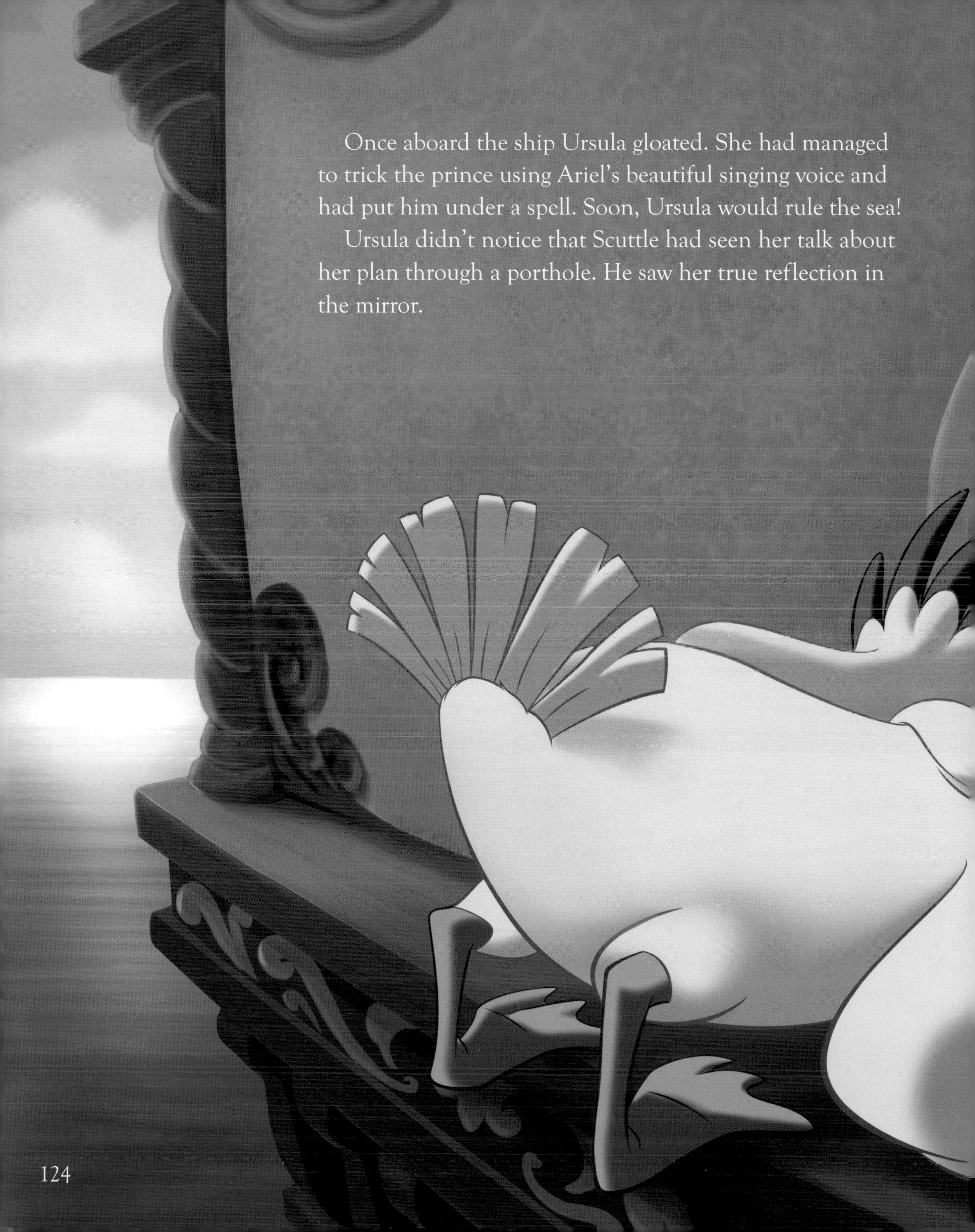

Scuttle flew back to tell Ariel that the girl that the prince was marrying was really Ursula the sea witch in disguise.

They had to stop the wedding! Ariel and her friends hurried to the ship. But the sun was going down. They had to move fast!

The wedding had already started when Ariel and her friends arrived at the ship.

Eric stood in a trance before the minister. Vanessa smiled to herself as they got closer to being married. She was sure that her plan was going to work. Ariel would be hers forever!

But just before Vanessa could say her vows all the animals that Ariel's friends had rounded up came to the rescue.

Scuttle managed to yank the necklace from Vanessa's neck and it smashed on the floor. Ariel's voice flowed back to her and Eric was released from the spell.

"You're the one!" exclaimed Eric as he heard Ariel's voice.

"You're too late!" laughed Ursula. The sun had set beneath the horizon and Ariel became a mermaid again.

Ursula changed back into her real form as the sea witch and dragged Ariel into the sea.

"I'm not going to lose her again!" shouted Eric as he went after Ariel.

Beneath the sea, King Triton appeared. “Ursula! Let her go!”

“She’s mine now,” Ursula replied, showing him Ariel’s contract. “We made a deal – but I might be willing to make an exchange.”

unto URSULA, the
Witch of the Sea...
,one voice,
for all eternity.
signed,
Ariel

To save his beloved daughter, Triton agreed to take Ariel's place. Now he would be Ursula's servant forever!

Ursula took the king's trident and stirred the waves, creating a huge whirlpool.

"Now I'm the ruler of all the ocean!" she declared as Ariel and Eric watched in horror.

Ursula grew and grew until she towered over the sea.

Eric saw an ancient sunken ship rising through the whirlpool and decided to climb aboard.

Just as Ursula took aim at him with her fiery trident he steered the jagged bow through the sea witch's heart.

The sea witch disappeared beneath the waves – her spell was broken. King Triton and all the poor, unfortunate souls Ursula had tricked were free at last!

But Ariel was a mermaid and Eric would always be a human. King Triton watched his daughter gaze longingly at her true love on the shore.

With a sigh, he touched his trident to the water and turned Ariel back into a human. The king smiled tenderly as he watched Ariel walk out of the sea to be with her one true love.

Some time later, Ariel's friends and family gathered to watch Ariel and Prince Eric get married. At last, she was part of the human world she loved. And she would live there happily ever after.

Disney Princess

Beauty and the Beast

Once upon a time, a spoiled, selfish prince lived in a castle in the forest. One night, an old beggar woman offered the prince a rose in return for shelter. Repulsed by her appearance, the unkind prince turned her away.

Suddenly, the old woman turned into an enchantress. She transformed the prince into a beast and placed a spell on the entire castle. To break the spell, the prince must learn to love – and be loved in return – before the last rose petal fell. Otherwise, he would remain a beast forever.

Not far away, a young woman named Belle lived in a small village. She dreamed of a more exciting life and wanted adventures like the ones in her favourite books.

Belle was very beautiful and had long been admired by Gaston, the most handsome and vain man in the village.

Gaston was certain that Belle would feel lucky to marry him. But Belle thought Gaston was rude and bad-mannered – and he didn't understand her love of books.

Belle returned home to find her father, Maurice, surrounded by pieces of his latest invention.

"I'll never get this bone-headed contraption to work!" said Maurice.

"Yes, you will," said Belle. "And you'll win first prize at the fair tomorrow."

With Belle's encouragement, Maurice quickly finished his automatic wood chopper. Then he loaded it on to a wagon and set out with his horse, Phillipe, for the fair.

Belle knew the villagers thought Maurice was odd, but he was her father and she always believed in him.

As evening fell, Maurice realized he had taken a wrong turn. He was lost, deep in the forest.

When wolves howled nearby, Phillipe threw Maurice off and bolted. The snarling wolves cornered Maurice in front of a huge gate. He banged on the gate until it opened, then gratefully stumbled inside.

Maurice crept into the enormous castle that lay beyond the gate. Before long, he heard voices whispering. He nervously picked up a candlestick to light his way.

"Hello!" said the candlestick.

Maurice couldn't believe his ears! All of a sudden, the castle seemed full of enchanted objects that could move and talk.

The candlestick, whose name was Lumiere, led Maurice to a comfortable chair in front of a warm fire.

Suddenly, a terrifying beast stormed into the room. "So you've come to stare?" the Beast growled.

"I meant no harm," Maurice stammered. "I needed a place to stay."

"I'll give you a place to stay," the Beast snarled. Then he locked Maurice in the dungeon.

Meanwhile, Gaston arrived at Belle's cottage. He announced that Belle's dreams were about to come true. He had made all of the preparations and planned for them to marry that very day!

"I'm very sorry, Gaston, but I don't deserve you," Belle replied. She opened the door and ...

... SPLAT! Gaston lost his balance on the way out and fell into a large, muddy puddle.

Gaston's sidekick, LeFou, stopped conducting the wedding band and asked Gaston what had happened.

Gaston was furious. "I'll have Belle for my wife, make no mistake about that!" he shouted.

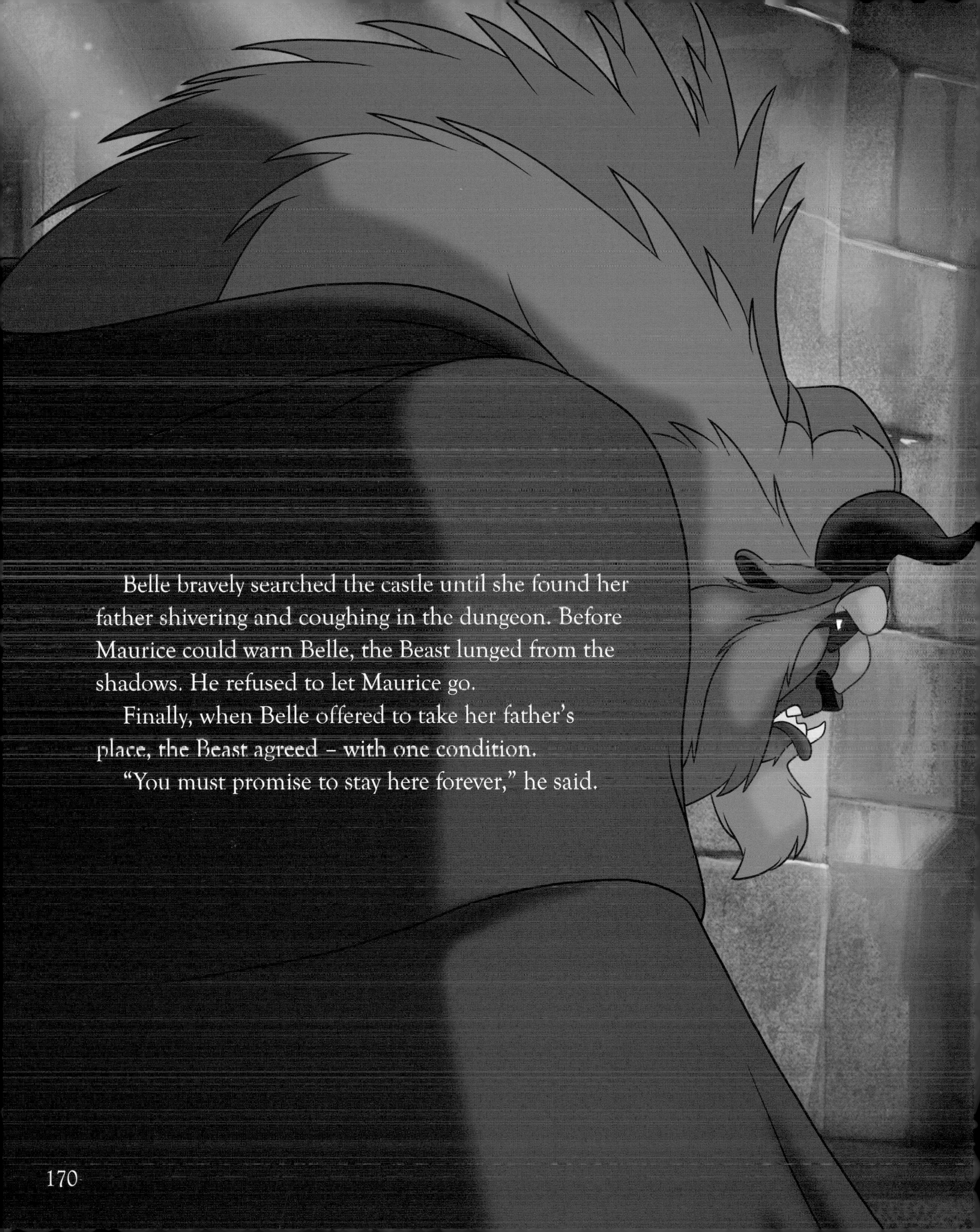

Belle bravely searched the castle until she found her father shivering and coughing in the dungeon. Before Maurice could warn Belle, the Beast lunged from the shadows. He refused to let Maurice go.

Finally, when Belle offered to take her father's place, the Beast agreed – with one condition.

"You must promise to stay here forever," he said.

Maurice raced back to the village, shouting for help to rescue Belle from a horrible beast. But no one believed him.

Meanwhile, Belle met some of the castle's enchanted servants, including a teapot called Mrs Potts, her son, Chip, and a clock named Cogsworth.

"That was a very brave thing you did," said Mrs Potts, thinking about how Belle had saved her father.

Belle refused to join the Beast for dinner. Instead, she waited until it was late, then crept down to the kitchen.

To Belle's delight, the staff treated her to a magnificent feast with singing and dancing. They were thrilled to finally have a guest!

After dinner, Belle wanted to explore the castle. The Beast had forbidden her to go into the west wing but Belle was curious. Although Cogsworth and Lumiere tried to discourage her, Belle slipped away from them and went up the stairs.

Belle peered into a dark room and gasped. Broken furniture and mirrors lay scattered as if someone had torn everything apart in a rage.

Then Belle saw a rose glowing under a glass dome. She noticed that several petals had fallen off. Entranced by its beauty, Belle reached out.

But before Belle could touch the rose, the Beast burst into the room.

"I warned you never to come here!" he bellowed. "Do you know what you could have done? Get out!"

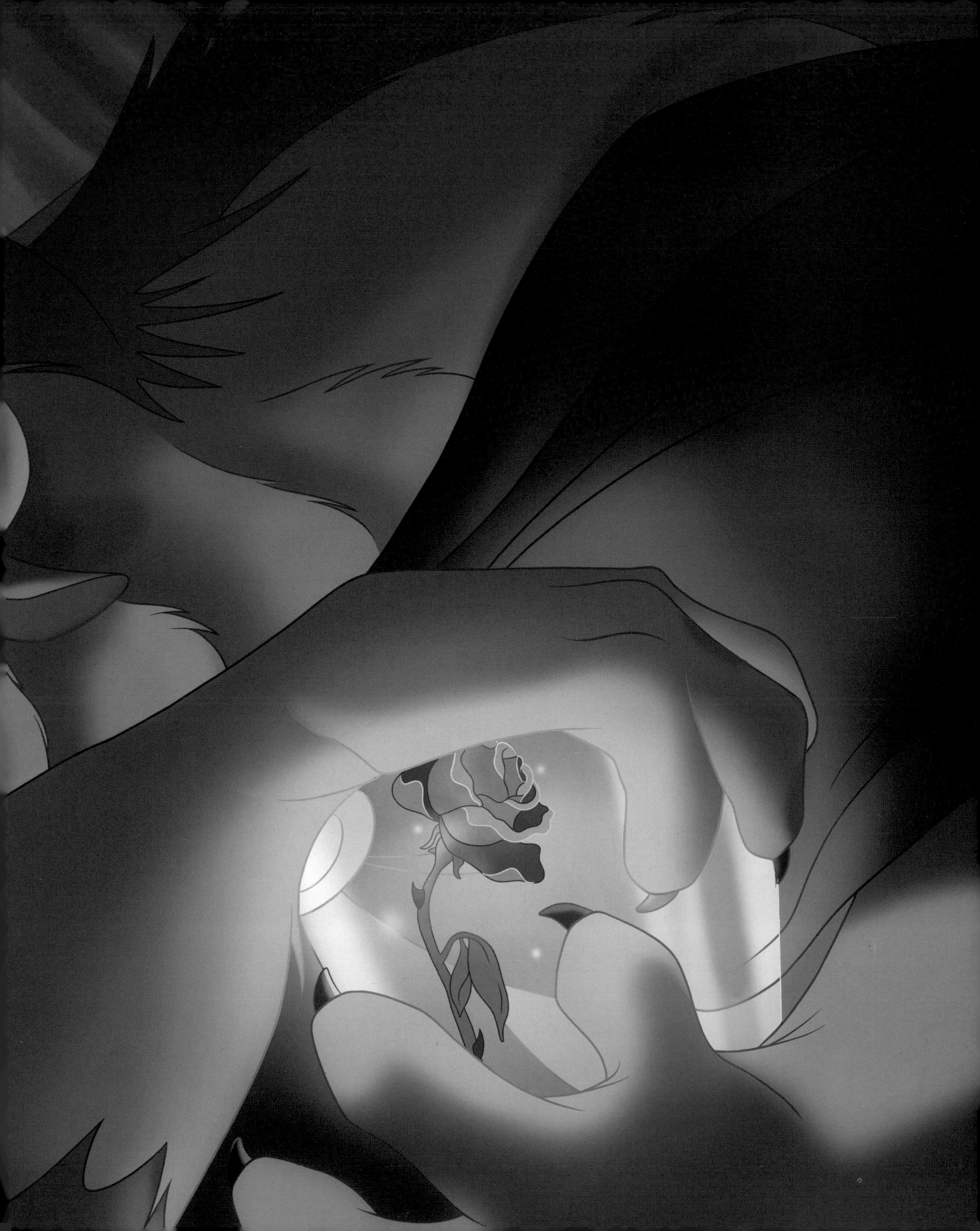

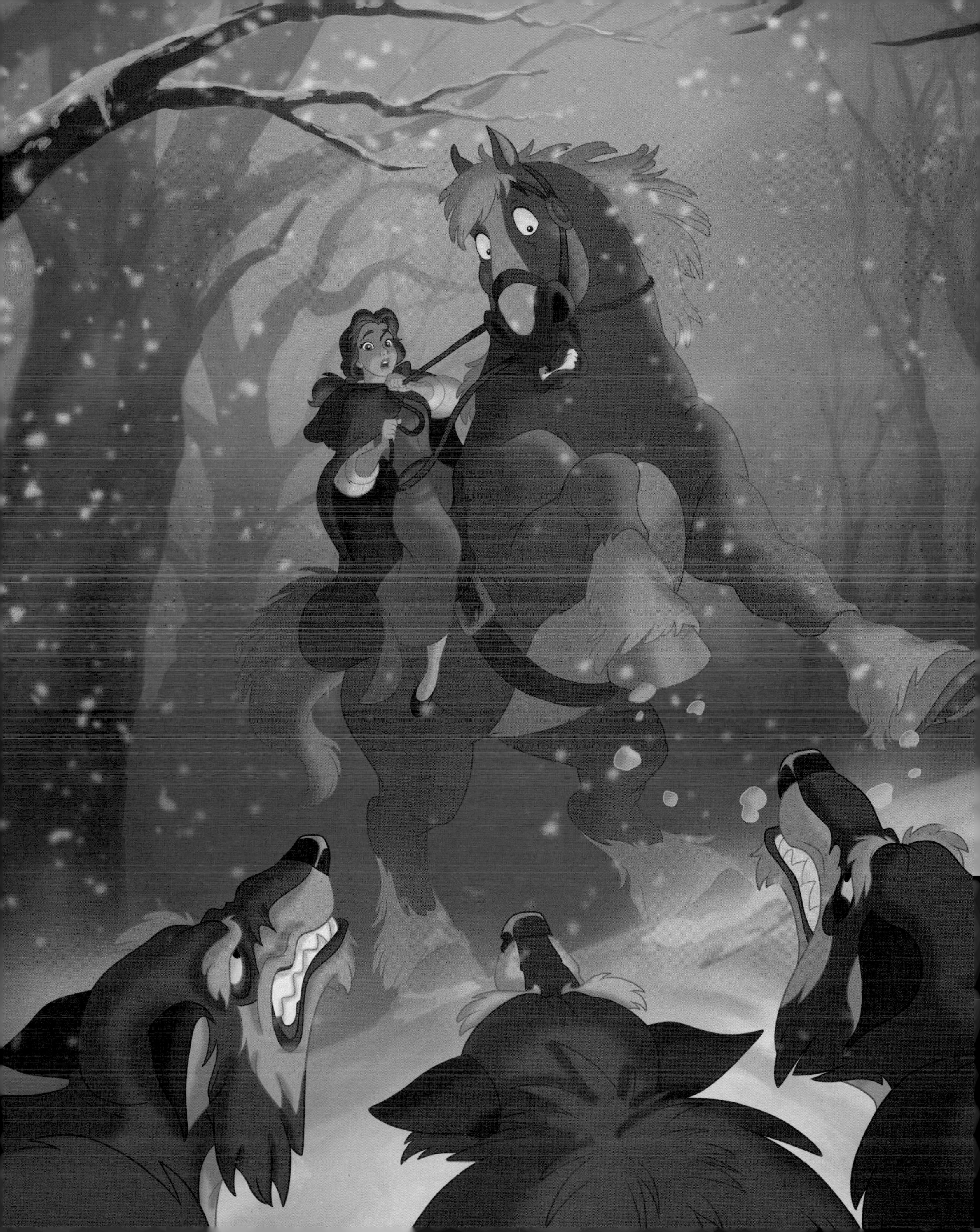

Terrified, Belle ran from the castle. “Promise or no promise, I can’t stay here another minute!” she cried.

She climbed on to Phillipe, who was waiting outside, and raced into the forest. Soon, they were surrounded by ferocious wolves.

Suddenly, the Beast sprang from the shadows. He fought off the wolves until Belle was safe. But the Beast had been injured.

Belle returned to the castle to help nurse the Beast's wounds.

"If you hadn't run away, this wouldn't have happened," he complained.

"If you hadn't frightened me, I wouldn't have run away," Belle replied. Then she added, "Thank you for saving my life."

"You're welcome," the Beast said quietly.

As the days passed, Belle began to see a different Beast. He was learning to be gentle and kind. Even little birds noticed the difference in him, perching on his shoulders and eating birdseed from his paws.

Everyone at the castle watched Belle and the Beast with hope. It seemed as if the pair were beginning to care for one another. Maybe – just maybe – the spell would finally be broken, and everyone would become human again.

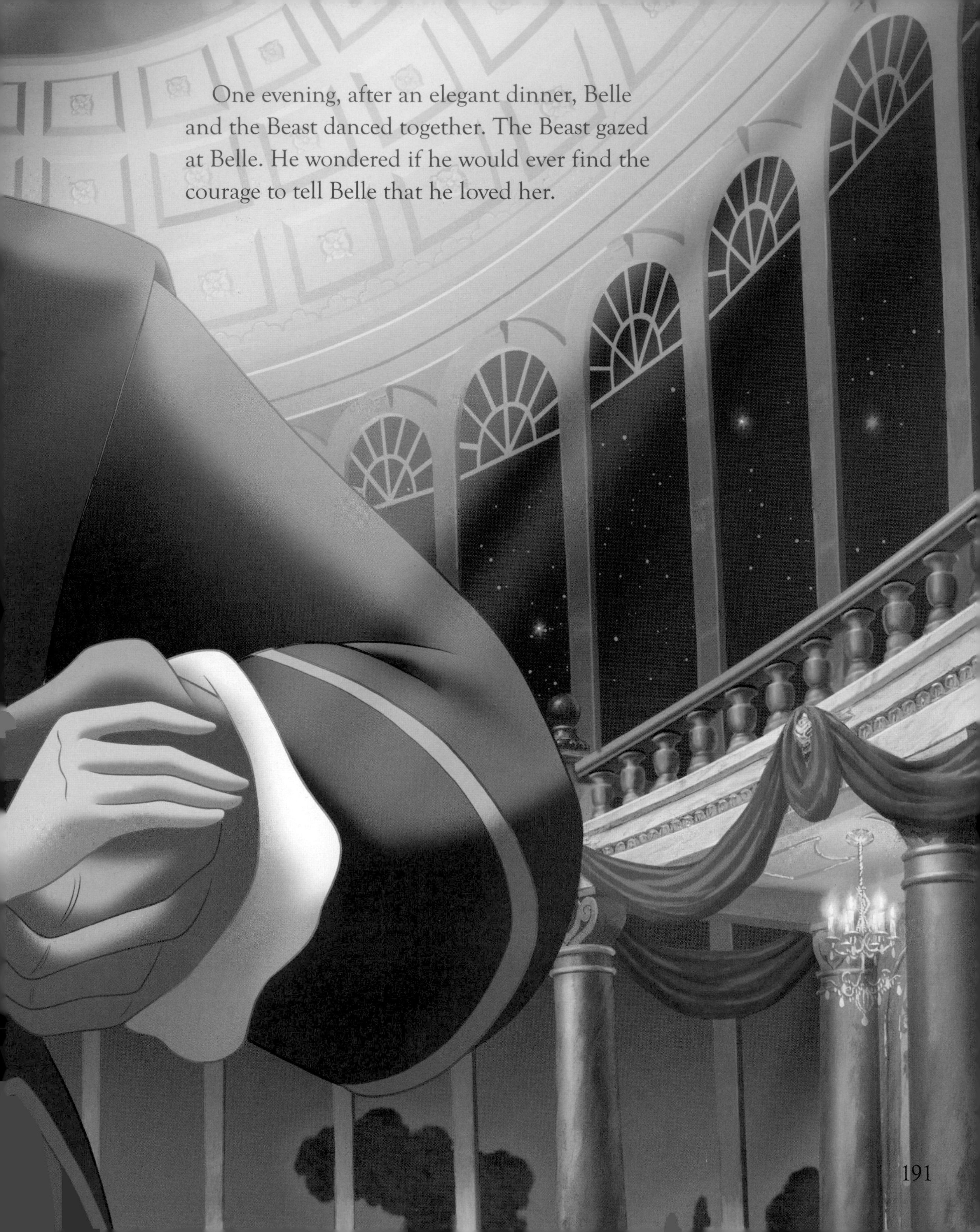

One evening, after an elegant dinner, Belle and the Beast danced together. The Beast gazed at Belle. He wondered if he would ever find the courage to tell Belle that he loved her.

The Beast knew how much Belle missed Maurice. He showed her a magic mirror, revealing an image of her father lost and trembling with cold as he desperately searched for Belle.

Sadly, the Beast released Belle from her promise and let her return home to her father. He gave Belle the mirror to remember him by.

With only one petal left on the enchanted rose, it seemed that any hope of breaking the spell was gone forever.

Belle rushed home to Maurice. To their surprise, Chip had sneaked into her bag and come along, too!

"How did you escape that horrible beast?" asked Maurice.

"He's different now, Papa," Belle said. But before she could explain, there was a knock at the door.

Gaston had bribed the owner of an asylum to declare Belle's father insane. Maurice would be locked up in the asylum – unless Belle agreed to marry Gaston!

As the guards dragged Maurice away, Gaston cornered Belle. "I might be able to clear up this little misunderstanding," he said slyly, "if you marry me."

"Never!" replied Belle.

To prove that her father wasn't crazy, Belle showed people the Beast's image in the magic mirror. "He's my friend," she told them.

Jealous and enraged, Gaston seized the mirror. "Kill the Beast!" he shouted.

Gaston locked Belle and Maurice in their cottage. Then he led a band of angry men to the castle.

BOOM! The doors shook as the mob tried to force their way into the castle.

With Belle gone, the Beast no longer cared about anything. "Just let them come," he said.

The servants tried to think of a plan.

When the angry mob stormed inside, the servants were ready! They fought and chased until the men ran away. Only Gaston remained.

Finding the Beast alone, Gaston raised his bow. When the arrow hit him, the Beast staggered back, crashing through the window and on to the castle roof.

Gaston followed the Beast outside and raised a club. Before he could strike, Belle screamed out from below, "No!" She and Maurice had escaped from the cottage and raced to the castle.

Startled, Gaston paused. The Beast heard Belle's voice, too, and was filled with hope. He suddenly found the strength to defend himself.

The Beast lunged at Gaston then decided to let him go. He climbed over to a terrace, where Belle had run to meet him.

All of a sudden, Gaston stabbed the Beast. He roared with pain and whipped around, accidentally knocking Gaston off the roof! Gaston plunged through the darkness as he fell to his death.

Belle pulled the Beast to safety and knelt beside him.

"You came back," he whispered. "At least I got to see you one last time."

"Please don't leave me," Belle sobbed. "I love you."

As Belle spoke, the last rose petal fell. Then, out of nowhere, magical sparkles began to swirl around the Beast. He rose into the air, turning slowly in a shower of light. Belle watched in disbelief as the Beast began to transform.

Magic swirled above the castle as the servants were transformed, too. The spell was broken!

"Belle!" cried the handsome prince. "It's me!"

Belle gazed into the prince's eyes. "It really is you!" she said in wonder.

Later, the servants watched as Belle and her prince waltzed across the ballroom.

"Are they going to live happily ever after?" Chip asked his mother.

"Of course, my dear," Mrs Potts replied.

And so they did.